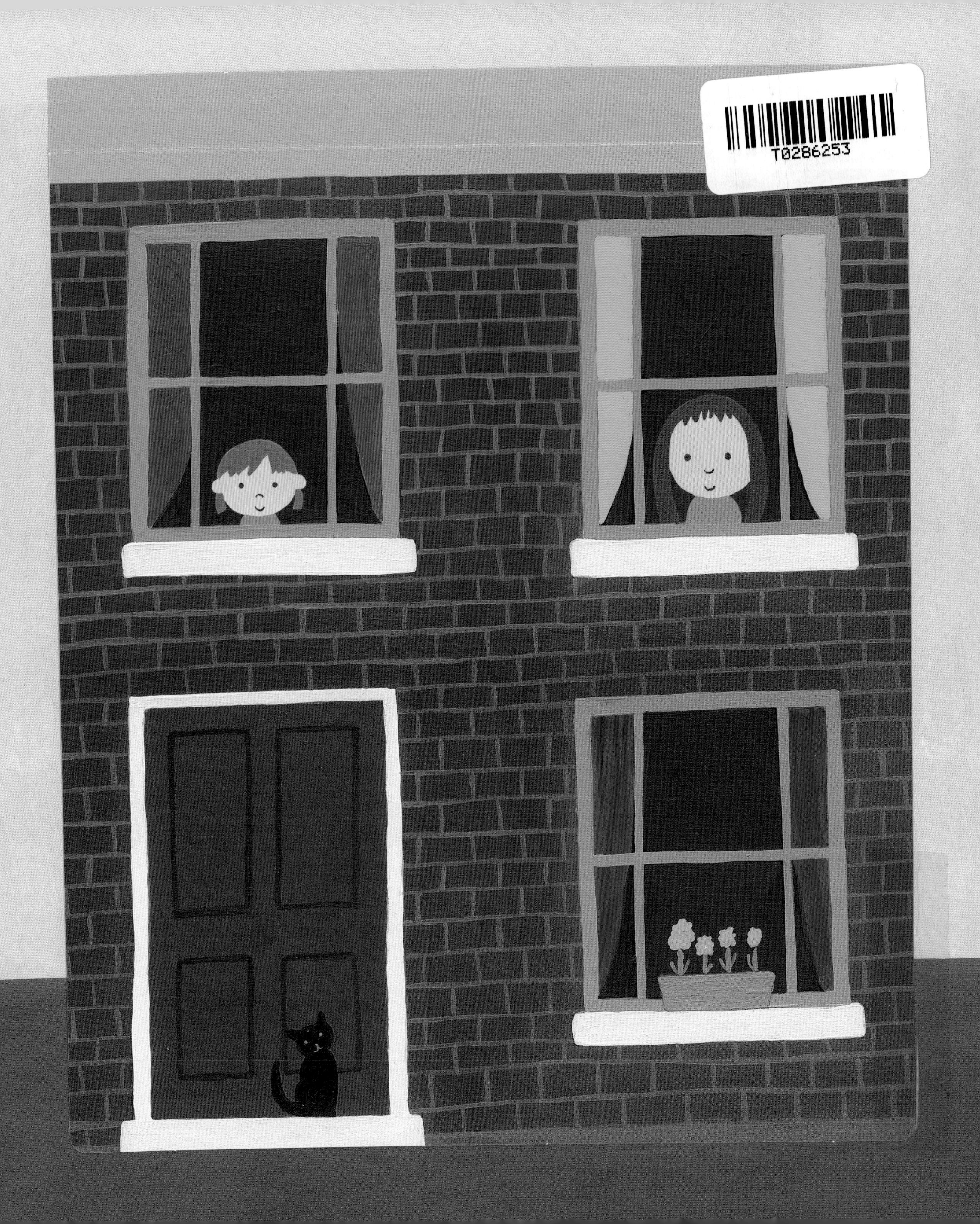

I have yellow walls in my
bedroom at my mom's house . . .

My mom and dad both know I don't like going to sleep in the dark. So at my mom's I have a panda night-light . . .

I keep some toys at my mom's house
and some at my dad's. . . .

My mom always used to pick me up from school.

Sometimes my dad takes me

camping on the weekend . . .

and sometimes my mom takes m

to see the animals at the farm.

when I was in
my school play . . .

On my birthday,
my mom made
me a cake . . .

If I miss my mom or my dad . . .

My mom and dad
love me a lot, and
so does everyone else
in my family.

Uncle Brian

Little Flora

Cousin Ruby